MR. MEN
ADVENTURE IN THE
JUNGLE

Original concept by
Roger Hargreaves

Written and illustrated by
Adam Hargreaves

EGMONT

Mr Dizzy had gone for a walk in the woods with all his friends.

But the further Mr Dizzy led his friends into the woods the more lost he became.

And then he came to a fork in the path and Mr Dizzy could not remember which way to go.

Should he take the left fork?

Or should he take the right one?

But the right one might be the wrong one.

So he turned left.

He and his friends walked and
walked and walked.

And then they walked some more.

The further they walked the denser the woods became.

"I don't think this is the woods any more,"
said Little Miss Wise.
"I think this is a jungle!"

"What makes you think that?"
asked Mr Dizzy.

"Because that is a gorilla!"
yelled Mr Jelly, quivering in fright.

"And there is an elephant!"
cried Little Miss Sunshine.

"And that is a tiger," pointed out Mr Strong.

"Oh dear," said Mr Dizzy. "We're lost in the jungle."

Suddenly, with an ear splitting roar, the tiger pounced.

Mr Strong leapt into its path and the tiger harmlessly bounced off him.

Running into Mr Strong is like running into a brick wall.

It hurts.

The jungle was so thick, and the vines were so tangled, and tree roots grew so close together that it was very difficult to make any headway at all.

It took all Mr Strong's strength to forge a track through the jungle.

And it was hot.

Hot and steamy.

Mr Dizzy's head was in a spin.

They must find their way home before it got dark.

And then night fell.

And it was not a very comfortable night for Mr Dizzy and his friends.

It was so noisy that they did not sleep a wink.

Even Mr Noisy thought it was too noisy.

The frogs croaked.

The crickets buzzed.

The insects clicked and chirped.

And the bats squeaked.

Things were no better in the morning.

In fact, they were decidedly worse.

A huge snake had wrapped its enormous coils around everyone.

Mr Jelly let out a muffled shriek.

It was Mr Daydream who came to the rescue. He whistled softly just like a flute and slowly he began to charm the snake until it was so sleepy and relaxed that everyone was able to escape from its embrace.

“Everything is so big in the jungle,” said Little Miss Tiny. “Even the butterflies are huge!”

“But they are beautiful,” added Little Miss Sunshine.

“And look at the size of that flower!” exclaimed Mr Nosey. “It’s gigantic. I wonder what it smells like?”

Mr Nosey stuck his long nose inside the huge flower.

"Ugh!" he cried. "It stinks!"

“How are we ever going to get out of here?” sighed Mr Nosey.

Little Miss Somersault glanced above her head.

“Look at the monkeys swinging through the trees,” she said. “Now, that’s the way to travel!”

And she was right.

Swinging from vine to vine was much easier.

Although, Mr Tickle did not need the vines!

They were travelling more quickly, but they were still lost. As lost as the lost city that they stumbled across. The city was a maze of passageways and corridors and steps that led down and stairs that led up with strange statues and eerie carvings.

They were well and truly lost in the lost city, that was lost deep in the jungle in the middle of nowhere.

In the middle of the lost city was a temple.

"If we climb the temple then we might see where we are," suggested Little Miss Wise.

The view was magnificent from the top and they could see for miles and miles in all directions.

They were not far from a river.

A river that would lead them out of the jungle.

On the riverbank they found some dug out canoes and began their journey home, paddling down the river.

"There are a lots of logs on this river," observed Mr Dizzy.

"Those are not logs, they are crocodiles!" shrieked Mr Jelly, quivering and wobbling. He quivered and wobbled so much that he overturned his canoe. SPLASH!

"Help!" he shrieked, as a large crocodile swam towards him with its mouth wide open showing its crooked yellow teeth.

Luckily, Mr Jelly had been sharing his canoe with Mr Noisy.

Mr Noisy opened his mouth as wide as the crocodile's mouth and let out an ear splitting shout.

It was as loud as a train roaring through a tunnel.

It was as loud as a jumbo jet taking off.

It was as loud as a pneumatic drill in a telephone box.

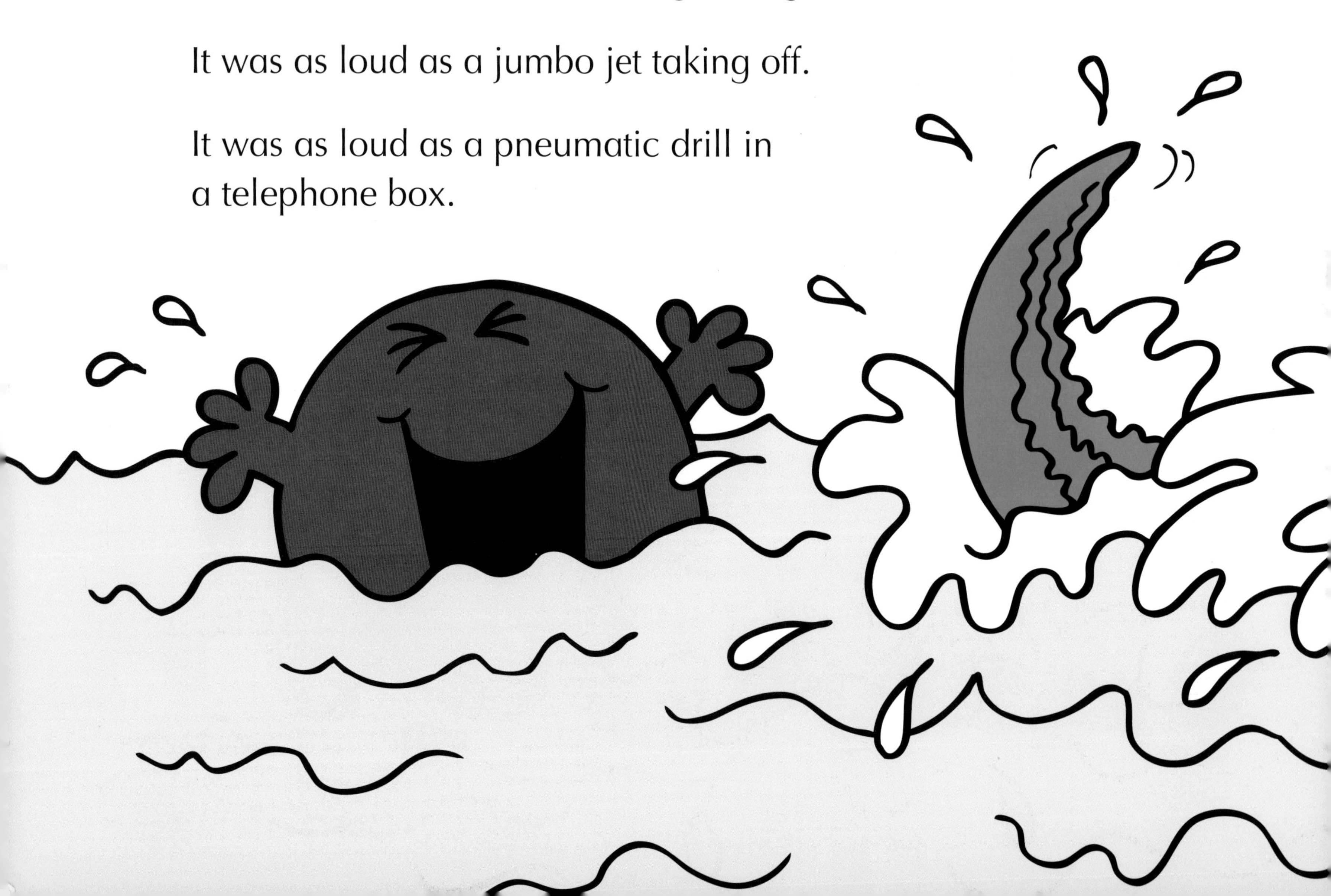

The crocodile leapt clear out of the water in fright and turned tail, frantically trying to swim away from this terrifying noise.

Mr Noisy grinned a big grin and he and Mr Jelly climbed back into their canoe.

It was a long paddle, but they did find their way back home.

It was much cooler at home.

And quieter.

And the insects were smaller.

And there were no tangled roots to trip them up.

And there were no dangerous animals that might eat them.

"What a relief," said Mr Dizzy.

And somewhere,
a very long way away,
deep in the jungle
a number of wild animals
also breathed a
collective sigh
of relief.